Peasy

The Potbellied Pig

SHARON THOMPSON

Published By: Sharon Thompson

ISBN 978-1-964452-61-6 (HardCover)
ISBN 978-1-964452-60-9 (SoftCover)
ISBN 978-1-964452-62-3 (Digital)

LCCN: 9781964452609

Printed in the United States of America

Sharon Thompson

Six year old Anya, her baby sister Aliyah, and her mom and dad visited Mrs. Porter's pig farm in June of 2023. At the time of the visit, a potbellied pig name Peasy followed them around.

Since then Anya wanted a potbellied pig for her pet.

Anya's mom and dad Mr. and Mrs. Dole, took note of Anya's interest and the way she interacted with the pigs.

Sharon Thompson

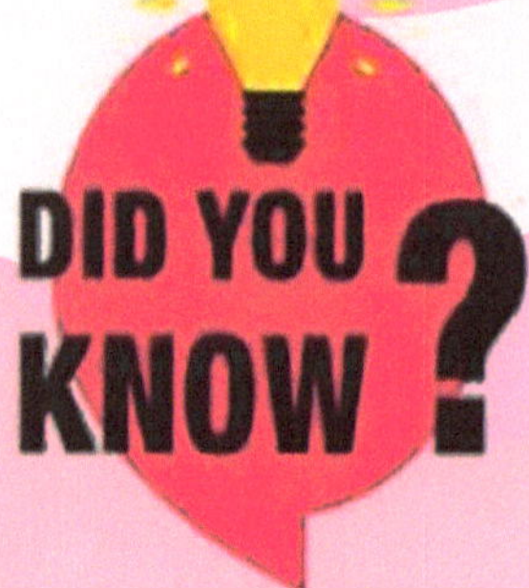

Potbellied pigs can be kept as pets! They're very smart—almost as clever as dogs.

Secretly, they arranged with Mrs. Porter to buy Peasy as a pet for Anya.

Few weeks later, Anya was pleasantly surprised when Mrs. Porter dropped Peasy off.

Peasy became Anya's Pride and joy. She called her the cool girl pig.

At times, Anya would sing to Peasy and tell her how special she was.

Pigs enjoy music too! Just like Peasy loved Disney songs, some pigs even have favorite tunes.

Anya was convinced that the Waltz Disney songs were Peasy's favorite. She said, "Peasy would close her eyes and nod when the Disney songs were Playing".

Anya and her parents would soon find out that Peasy was no ordinary potbellied pig. Peasy was very funny and very smart.

Sharon Thompson

Early one Friday morning in October, Anya and her family left home to visit their aunt Tracey. It was that very morning Peasy funny side came out.

FEARLESS

Because they did not get far

Before Peasy drove Anya's electric toy car

She drove it so fast, shouting she was having a blast

She drove into Mr. and Mrs. Dole's room

While humming a Waltz Disney tune

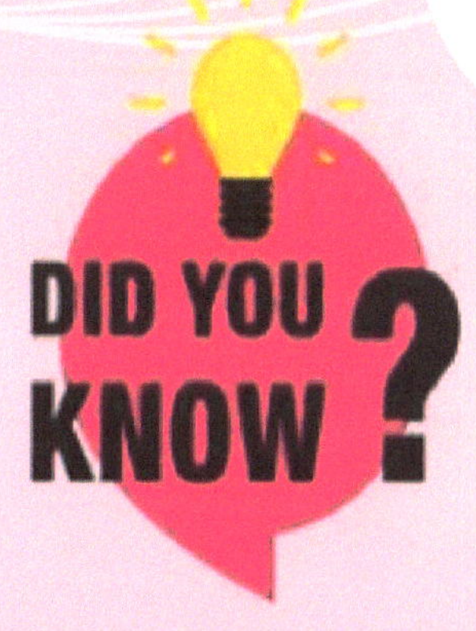

Pigs are quick learners. Scientists taught pigs to play simple video games—so Peasy driving a toy car isn't too far-fetched!

Sharon Thompson

The first thing in the room that caught Peasy's attention

Was Mrs. Dole's fashionable wig collection

Peasy tried on five of Mrs. Dole's nine wigs

While she sang and danced a few jigs

Pigs are super curious. They like to explore new things—so trying on wigs and necklaces is something a playful pig might actually do!

She tried on Mrs. Dole's necklace made from freshwater pearls

Meanwhile she twisted and twisted and then twirled

She looked at herself in the mirror wearing the long brown wig

And said, "Hmm, hmm, hmm, this awesome brown wig

Surely looks good on this potbellied pig"

Alexa told Peasy to explain hmm, hmm, because she did not understand

Peasy froze for a minute, staring at Alexa on the nightstand

Peasy ran into Anya's room and jumped in her bed

Where she laid for a while and rest her frightened little head

Few minutes later, she said she was no longer afraid

Of that thing that made her utterly dismayed

Peasy got very curious; she wanted to know what Alexa was about

She went back into Anya's parent's room, saying she got to check it out

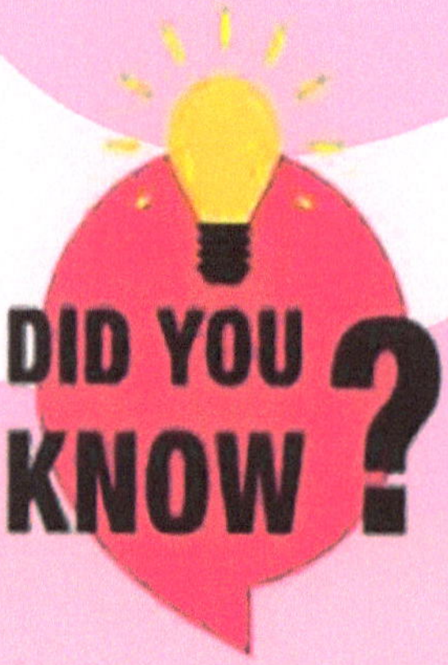

Pets often get confused by voice assistants like Alexa. Dogs, cats, and even pigs sometimes bark, squeal, or stare at the "mystery voice."

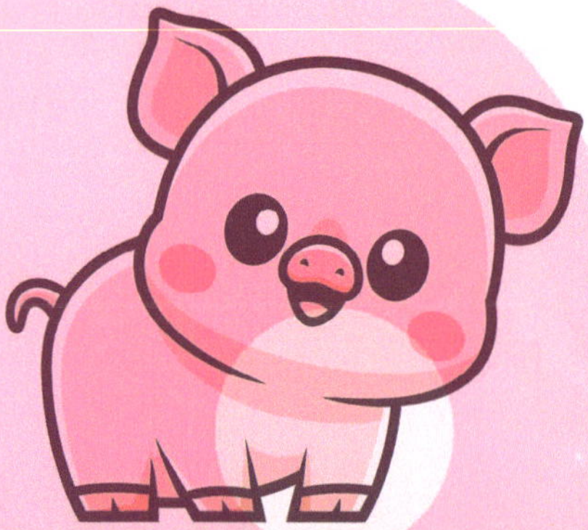

Before she went back into Mr. and Mrs. Dole's room

She made sure she armed herself with a broom

Yet her heart beat fast and was full with fear

She whispered to herself, hoping Alexa would not hear

But Alexa said to Peasy, "Speak a bit louder and clearer my dear"

Peasy squealed loudly, "This thing is no fun".

She dropped the broom and started to run

She ran out of the room and jumped into Ali-yah's high chair

She squealed for a minute wishing Anya was there

Not very long after she fell asleep in the chair

Mr. Wally backed his truck up, and it started to beep

That woke Peasy up from her very light sleep

She said she was happy to get at least five minutes' sleep

Because that Alexa thing sure gave her the creeps

CHEVY

Sharon Thompson

It started to rain, heavy pouring rain

Peasy went out in the pouring rain

Saying when it rains, she has much to gain

She dug in the wet dirt with her little pink snout

Mr. Wally's dog watched, wondering what the digging was about

Sharon Thompson

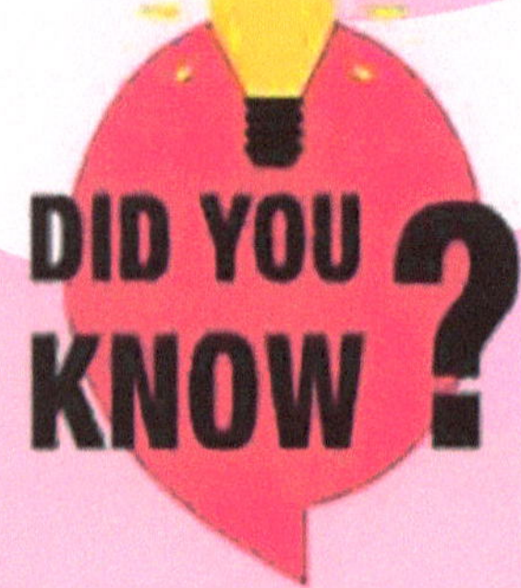

Pigs don't sweat! That's why they roll in mud—it keeps them cool, protects their skin, and works like sunscreen.

She dug for awhile until she made a pile of mud

Then she rolled over and over in the mud to cool off

The mud felt good to Peasy; she shook her head and laughed

Peasy soon realized something was on the prowl

She feared it was a bear, she listened for a growl

The thing hid behind a humongous tree

For Peasy's dear life, she wanted to flee

Sharon Thompson

Mr. Wally's dog barked at a flying lark

At that moment, Peasy thought to herself barking was not smart

She really, really hoped the thing behind the tree was not a bear

Luckily for her it was a huge buck, a male reindeer

She went back inside to clean off the mud

She headed straight to her beloved Anya's bathtub

She turned on the water and made it flow

Thinking to herself, no one would ever know

She poured in the bath some shower gel

She chuckled and said, the gel would clean her body well

Peasy slid in the bathtub and started to scrub

Moving around until she made a lot of suds

Meanwhile she continued to scrub, scrub, scrub

Sharon Thompson

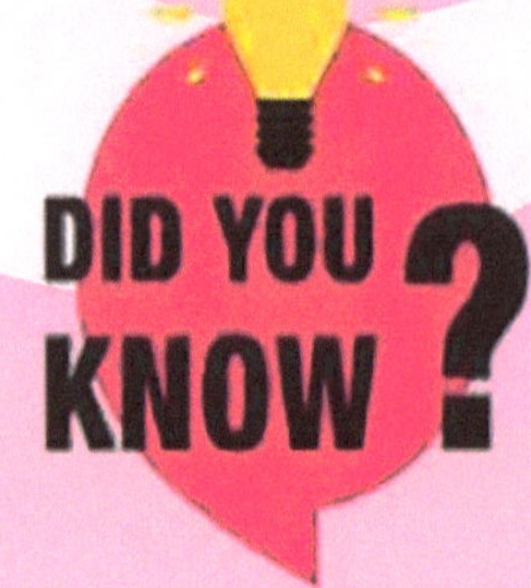

Pigs enjoy water and baths. A bubble bath like Peasy's might sound funny, but pigs do like splashing around!

She laughed a good laugh, then said it was good to be home alone

She was clueless that she was watched on the Doles' cell phones

When she found out, she was very much ashamed

Peasy really thought she was on top of her game

For a minute she felt like she was a victim

To be watched by the Doles' security system

But she laugh and said it did a good job

Even if it told on a miniature potbellied hog

Sharon Thompson

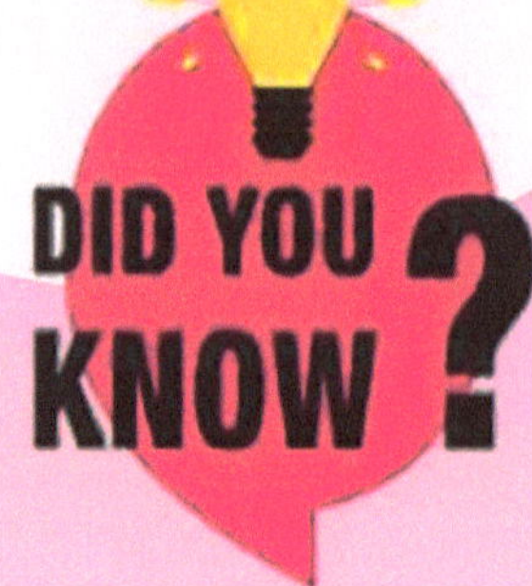

Pets are often caught on home cameras doing silly things. Some pigs have even become internet stars.

Peasy made the right choice and quickly apologized

Anya told Peasy she was funny and smart

And that she missed her when they were apart

She then rubbed Peasy's head

Soon after, they both went to bed

THE END

Sharon Thompson

PEASY'S
ACTIVITY PAGES

"Peasy wants to find Anya! Can you help her get through the maze to reach her best friend?"

Instructions: A simple squiggly path maze. Start: Peasy on one side. End: Anya smiling on the other.

Instructions:

"Peasy loves rolling in the mud! Use your favorite crayons or markers to color her and the big mud puddle."

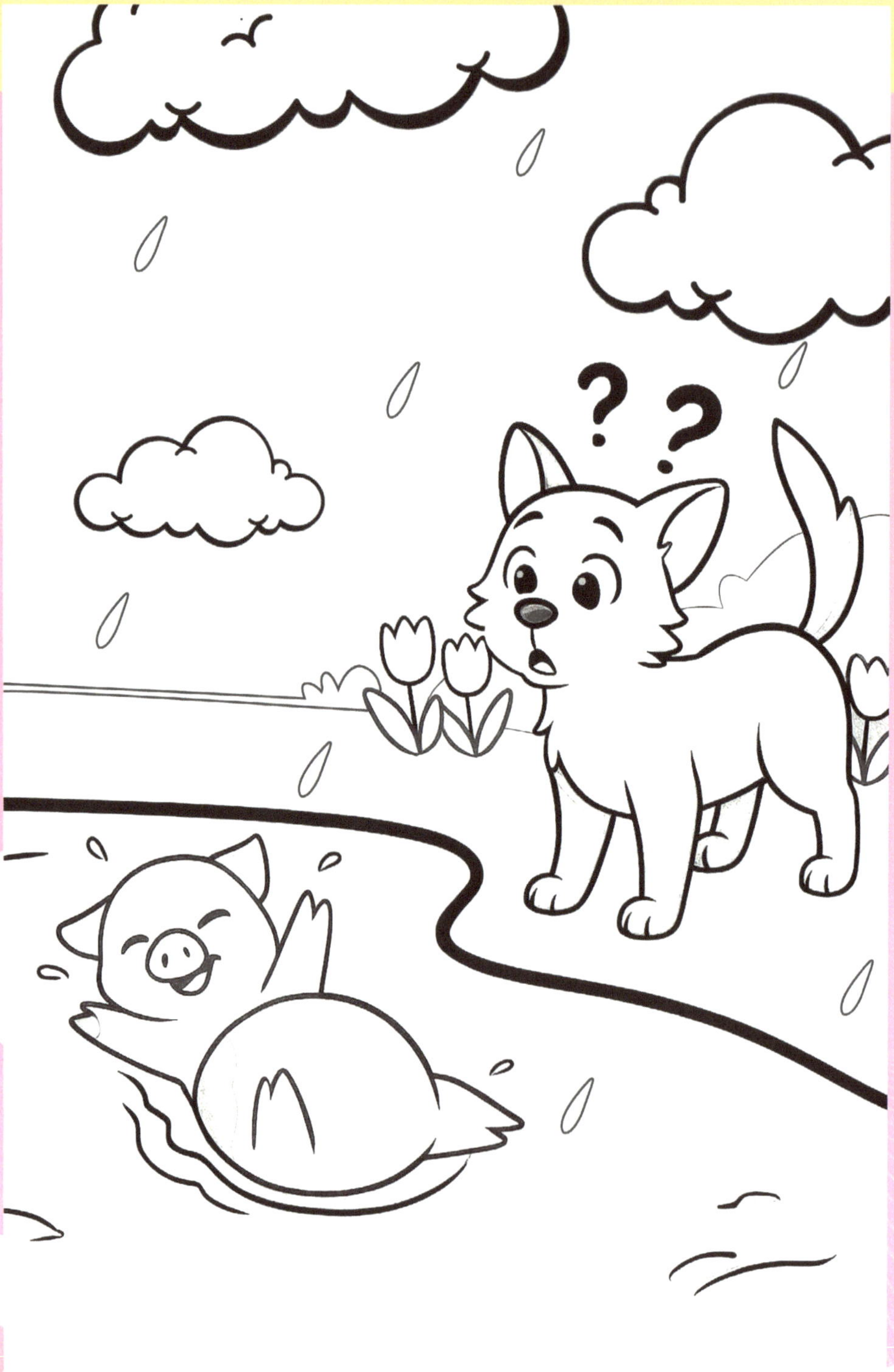

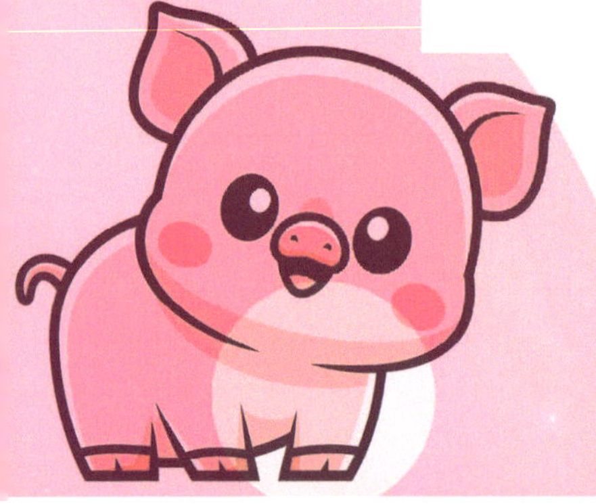

PEASY THE POTBELLIED PIG
Find the words in the word search

R	L	T	G	A	W	E	C	R	G	O	D	E	R
S	A	R	O	O	N	I	R	Y	A	X	E	L	A
W	I	L	T	T	N	I	A	R	O	R	O	R	E
I	M	M	U	U	P	L	B	A	T	I	E	H	G
A	I	M	D	W	E	O	T	R	M	T	T	R	L
N	E	U	G	I	W	Y	D	E	R	A	A	U	T
P	U	D	A	H	E	P	O	O	B	S	D	T	I
R	G	C	S	A	P	I	P	T	D	O	L	E	P
N	K	A	G	Y	L	G	D	I	S	N	E	Y	Y
N	C	R	G	I	E	S	T	E	E	W	S	H	P
N	U	C	C	L	O	H	O	I	N	E	X	I	W
I	R	P	K	A	T	U	Y	N	P	G	I	H	N
T	T	L	W	A	L	L	Y	G	G	T	G	R	S
S	A	Y	N	A	P	E	A	S	Y	I	X	M	H

ANYA	DOLE	MUD	BATH
ALIYA	WALLY	CAR	TOY
PEASY	DOG	DISNEY	ALEXA
PIG	TRUCK	SONG	TREE
PORTER	WIG	RAIN	

ANSWER KEY

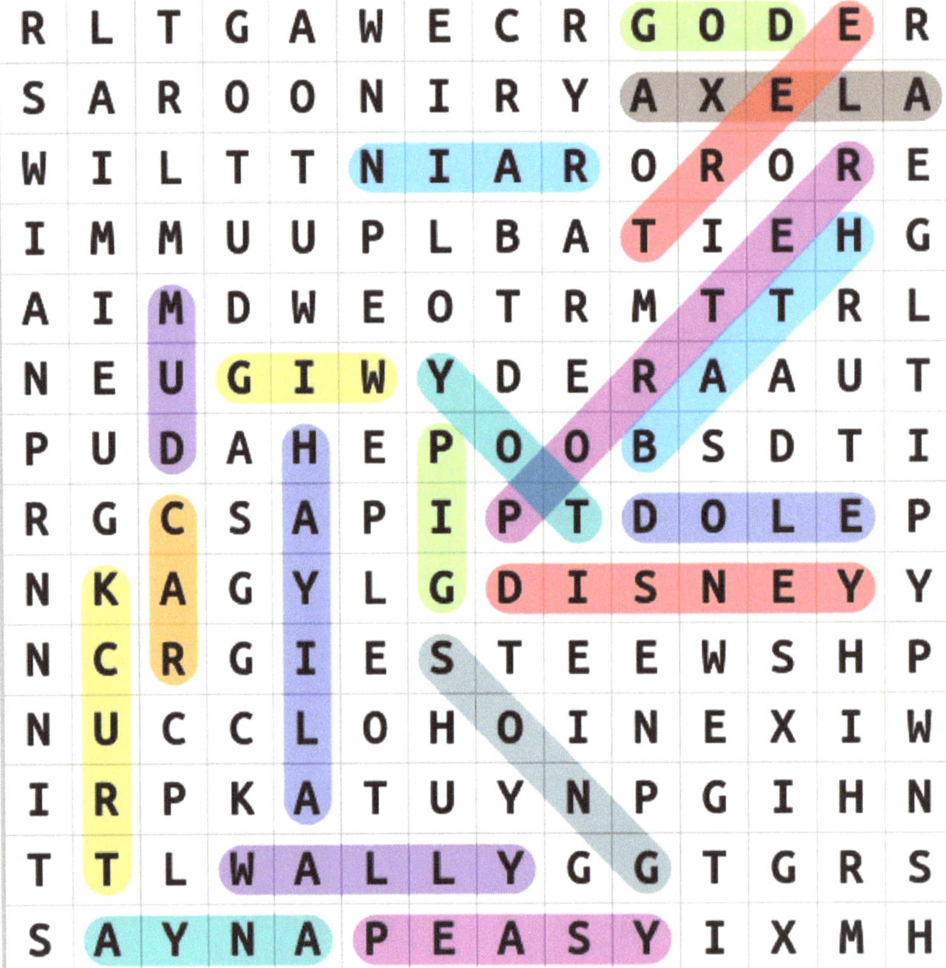

ANYA   DOLE   MUD   BATH
ALIYA   WALLY   CAR   TOY
PEASY   DOG   DISNEY   ALEXA
PIG   TRUCK   SONG   TREE
PORTER   WIG   RAIN

54